Sweet and Fiery Erotic Love Poems

Romantic Poetry

RIVER STONE

ISBN: 978-1-7774442-0-4

DEDICATION

To my husband
Thank you for your love and support
Lover boy toot your horn!

CONTENTS

FOREWORD

Sweet and Fiery Erotic Love Poems are perfect for creating moods.

Emotions will be ignited and bodies will be charged. Warm fuzzy feelings will engulf you but what you do next is totally up to you.

Keep your love alive and the fire burning!

PART ONE

LOVE

Fall in love and love with all of your being!

MY QUEEN

I worship her with my stare
She is my precious queen
And love her fiercely like there is no
tomorrow
With my entire being
-River Stone

LET ME SHARE YOUR LIFE

Let me share your life
Every day month and year
I will dry your tears
Clouds will be chased away
Tell me your silly jokes
As laughter fills our days

I want to dance with you
As we sing our favorite song
Tell me about your day
While I rub your feet
Whisper your fantasies
They will be fulfilled
I will cherish you my love
Just let me share your life

-River Stone

FOREVER

Many seek love each day
with you I have found so much
My lover my friend
beautiful inside and out
Your love is amazing
my heart sings
With you I am comfortable
and at ease

When you smile
I get warm cozy feelings
Your kisses cause
my knees to wobble
My love for you grows each day
You are my special gift
I treasure
I will always be there for you
it's my commitment

You bring joy and laughter
sun or rain
I want to continue
on this amazing journey
With you forever
                -River Stone

MY AWESOME LOVE

I remember the first time we met
You still make me smile
and ignite my fire
My heart beats with love for you
what I feel is truly magical
My awesome love I am yours
and you are mine always
I love when you stare at me
your eyes twinkling with glee

Sweetie you are the shoulder
that I lean on, my sturdy rock
You give the best medicine
laughter each day
You make it easy for me
to share my hopes and dreams
With you hand in hand I find
balance
Sweet memories, today joy
tomorrow more splendor

My awesome love
there is no one like you
You are perfect for me
  -River Stone

MY HEART SINGS

I love to see you smile at me
It makes my heart sings
You are perfect the way you are
Beautiful charming and sweet
When we walk hand in hand
I am reminded of how lucky I am
We have experienced challenges
But they always pull us closer
The depth of our love so true
Happy times I will always treasure
-River Stone

DESTINY

Nothing compares
to being in love with you
By your side is where I will always
be
No longer blue just a colorful
rainbow
I am in paradise secured in your
love
Amazingly with you I can be myself
Hold me close as I float in wonder
Tell me your wants needs and
desires
I will spend a lifetime
fulfilling each one
-River Stone

SWEET LOVE

Longing for someone to complete me
Then I find you as darling as can be
Fall in love under the rainbow
Wonderful sun after the rainfall
You are so beautiful inside and out
Flawless like fresh summer daisies

Nervous expectations when I am
with you, your eyes twinkle makes
me topsy-turvy
I wonder what our life together will
be, your love is assurance of our
journey
When your smile frames your cute
face, I am convinced this is more
than love
My body shudders when you are
near, in your arms I am hook
defenselessly
The keeper of my heart I give to you
Hope you love me even more
tomorrow
Beautiful and faithful our sweet
bond, my lifetime desire is forever
with you
-River Stone

REMINISCING

As I stared into the sunset
I am reminded of her auburn hair
The raging waves lapped at my feet
Not quite as feisty as my queen
Tiny pebbles scattered in the sand
Smooth as her skin with curves like
hers

A pair of palm trees towered tall
Made me ached to touch her long
legs
I ordered a Bloody Mary from the
bar
And tasted her plummy cherry lips
The warm evening air hugged me
tight
Eyes closed I enjoy being in her
arms
A bird sang and I am lost in her
song
Madly in love I reminisced by the
sea

-River Stone

LOVE ME

Smile at me
and my lips will curve upwards
Kiss me
I will drink and share my sweetness
Hold me
and my arms will surround you
Dance with me
and I will match each and every step
Touch me
I will share my body and soul with
you
Love me
and I will be yours forever

-River Stone

OPEN YOUR PETALS

Open your petals for me dearest
I want to savor your sweet perfume
Open your petals for me sweetie
let me caress your softness

Open your petals for me darling
let me taste your nectar
Open your petals for me honey
my tongue will lick your dew drops

Open your petals for me sugar-pie
so, my fingers can enter your folds
Open your petals for me lover
let me stroke and pleasure your bud

Let me play a song on your leaves
and spill my water at your root
Let me cause you to spill seeds
and form sucklings

Open your petals for me beautiful
we'll dance in the wind, in our
garden

-River Stone

LOVE FLOWS DEEP

My love for you flows deep
You infuse my heart with warmth
You bring the sun and rainbow
Tears fade away and smiles stay
Your kisses sweet as honeysuckle

Your touch brings shivers and
thrills
Passionate tremor whenever we join
You are the nut to my bolt
The paddle to my canoe
Fulfillment as we ride
      -River Stone

SWEET FLOWER

Fascinating beauty
you captivate my thoughts
Your sweet rosy smell
saturates my head
Your aura causes
my heart to skip beats

Smooth silky skin
I yearn to touch
Love it when
your mouth curves upwards
While those alluring eyes
stare at me
You taste like cinnamon honey
I salivate at the thought
of kissing you
Your honeyed voice heats my body
Each of your stroke
caress my inner desires
Dew flows uncontrollably
like my love for you
                -River Stone

GIRL OF MY DREAMS

You winked and fiddled with your
hair
My smile was beaming as I flirt back
You asked the waiter to send over a
beer
And I waved for you to join me at my
table

Funny charming confident and sexy
I was intoxicated with your beauty
You were chatty while I sipped my
drink
Best of all was you asking for my
number

The script flipped you played hard to
get
During the chase you captured my
heart
Girl of my dreams you are such a
tease
Playful and loving in and out of the
sheet

-River Stone

I FELL IN LOVE THAT NIGHT

I fell in love that night
it was under the stars
Mist drenched air
under your piercing stare

I fell in love that night
moonlight caressed our faces
As the sound of our racing
hearts broke the silence

I fell in love that night
the wind whistled a sweet song
You held me tight as I shivered
from the chill of the night

I fell in love that night
we enjoyed the sweet garden aroma
You whispered naughty fantasies
and made me slippery and wet

I fell in love that night
you pledged that this was forever
You loved my imperfections
and for countless more reasons
I fell in love with you that night
and it was reciprocated

-River Stone

SEEDS OF LOVE

We planted the seeds of love
And watered the buds with joy
Roots have now anchored down
Fed and nurtured by our love
Leaves enfolded in the sunshine
Cherished we formed a lustrous
bond
Flowers bloomed as happiness grew
Thorns removed our love came alive

-River Stone

LET ME MAKE IT RIGHT

This is real you are leaving me
after my countless indiscretions
Patient and tolerant so forgiving I
take you for granted
My pure gem I don't want to lose
you, I hurt deeply
The hollow feeling rips through me
please come back let me make it
right

Yes, I am a cheating sneaky load of
filth, you call it and I admit
Always looking for more when all I
need is you
I know this is unforgivable
but I am pleading let me make it
right

I see the hurt in your eyes
deep within your soul
Foolish must be my middle name
thinking you will always be here
Forgive me for destroying us
give me one more chance to make it
right

My sobs echo in the empty space

missing you is my new anthem
You are the best thing in my life
My heart bleeds, it's you I love
I beg you let me make it right
-River Stone

YOU ARE MY EVERYTHING

You are my morning cup of tea
a few sips and I am with glee
You are the reason I get out of bed
to share another amazing day
You are the ray of sunshine
that fills me with happy thoughts
You are the compass when I feel lost
guiding my direction

You are the gentle breeze on
a hot day keeping me comfortable
You are my warm fluffy coat
protecting me from the chill
You are the sweet song that fills my
head makes me dance and sing
You are my everything and much
more my sweet darling

-River Stone

BEYOND A LIFETIME

Your picture is painted in my mind
filling my thoughts my every dream
Tiny strokes of a brush expose your
beauty
Effortlessly the canvas comes alive
with radiance of your bold colors
Divine and charming inside and out
I am in a daze
Tracing your palm, our fingers
entwine and I feel your warmth

My art gallery only displays your
amazing pieces
You are unique my priceless
treasure
Eyes open or close you are with me
I am engulfed with joy invested
in our love
Each shapely contour perfectly
painted
Your vivacious spirit intuitively
captured
I am your biggest admirer
number one fan
If you could see you how I do
you would know that
I will be loving you

beyond a lifetime

-River Stone

22

beyond a lifetime

-River Stone

SOME THINGS ARE MEANT TO BE

Beaming with happiness
every day with you is a gift
Patience is a virtue and
some things are meant to be

You come to me a little guarded
determine to protect your heart
You cautiously remove barriers
and my humble patience pays off

I fall in love with the true you
that was revealed
Your dashing smile couple with a
little bit of sweet shyness
Love your silly jokes and your
appreciation of the simple things

It excites me when we walk in the
street
And you take my hand for the world
to see
You are strikingly attractive but
more remarkably is how you love
and care for me
My heart does cartwheels when you
are near
Undeniable is our powerful

chemistry
When we touch it's a scorching
blaze
Our souls collide
some things are truly meant to be
                              -River Stone

COME BE WITH ME

I am restless like the choppy sea
when you are not near
Come spend your days with me
let me kiss your crimson lips
Stay, stay don't go yonder
your absence will make
my lonely heart wonders

I need you pressed against me
to feel the warmth of your body
Come bury the longing that
consumes me
You are the missing piece to my
eternity
You are my true love
I want to be wrapped up in your
heat
Come lets us fuel the fire
then extinguish the blaze of our
desire

-River Stone

PART TWO
SENSUAL

To desire and be desired always!

DREAMY

Dreamy eyed she stares at me
Tousled hair all over the pillow
Here comes her honeyed smile
As she basked in the afterglow
-River Stone

MY ENDLESS LOVE

My senses awake under your gaze
Life is complete with you in it
We have weathered many storms
The result a stronger bond
I admire your kind caring way
My heart is yours until the end
With your smile my heart flutters
Your whisper makes me shiver
Stroke of your fingers drive me wild
Whenever we explode, I am in heaven
You are my endless love

-River Stone

CAN'T GET ENOUGH OF YOUR LOVE

I can't get enough of you my love
Together so long
I still want you need you
It excites me when
you melt under my touch
Kissing your lips
stroking your satin skin
Your sweet voice
a note to a song

You are a divine and
grand beautiful soul
My love you are
my treasure I will cherish
The way you respond
when I enter your fold
It is my pleasure
when you moan and groan
I will take you
over the cliff some more
The connection
a celebration of our love
                -River Stone

DREAMS COME TRUE
I love waking up next to you
Pulling you closer
before we get out of bed
Your tousled hair and sleepy smile
Warms eyes looking back at me
You are my evidence
that dreams come true

Sweet smart beautiful and sexy
You warm my heart
when you are near
Stirs my loin with just a stare
I want you need you more and more
Crushed against your sweet softness
Lost in your tight heat
Riding the waves then
relishing in the afterglow
-River Stone

FEVER

Feverish under your touch
Cool me with your tongue
Oh goodness not the effect
Now I am a raging furnace
More strokes my blood boils
Aching I swim in hot lava
Here comes the explosion
Flood of juices, ahhhh
finally, the cool down
-River Stone

GIFT EXCHANGE

Lover here is my gift to you and only
you
It is thick and hard with a rim at the
top
Generous in length with jewels at
the base
It will give you wild rides and
endless fun
In exchange I accept your sweet
treasure

So soft smooth slippery and wet
I will enjoy the heat and snug tight
grip
Sure, it will lead to breathlessness
And will blow my mind and leave me
spent
These are perfect gifts wrapped in
our love

-River Stone

CANDLELIGHT

I love the flicker of the candlelight
casting shadows on your handsome
face
Just enough light for me to see
your loving sweet expression
Each flicker electrifying the mood
bodies are already in heat

Remove my garments
and touch me where the rose is red
Free me like a monarch butterfly
let me spread, I promise I won't fly
away
This is where I want to be
sandwiched against your hardness

Let your fingers and lips do the
talking
Oh yes bring on the raging heat
Ride me like a pony
do not gallop I want you slow and
steady
My preference is the long distance
I crave multiple orgasms

Stroke me in ways I desire

each and every part of me
Spill your water and
cool my sweltering pot
Hold me close until the candle
burns low
                    -River Stone

I WONDER

I wonder if I kiss you
Will you shiver in my arms?

I wonder if I lick you
Will you surrender to my tongue?

I wonder if I make love to you
Will you lose control?

I wonder how you would react
Would you melt under my touch?

I wonder if I fondle your flower
Will you clench on my fingers?

I wonder if I enter your abyss
Will you have an orgasm?

I wonder if I confess my love
Will you love me in return?

-River Stone

BARED WITH YOU

Peel off my covers
Then remove your wrapper
Birthday suits are preferred
I want to be bare under you
Take a ride on top of you
Form a spoon with you
Enjoy a banana split with you
Play the doggy with you
Legs on shoulders with you
Then explode with you
For a lifetime with you
      -River Stone

SEXTING

Ping!
I am hollow
when you are not here
Raging anxiety
to have you near
I want to be
in your embrace
As you plug
my tight space

You are my stallion
I am your cowgirl
When I crack my whip
It's time to accelerate
Let me ride you to the gorge
to see fireworks on the other side
Hurry on over
I am wearing only cowgirl boots
                    -River Stone

PART THREE
EROTIC

Be passionate about satisfying and being satisfied every time!

PLAY FOR ME

She climbs on top of
the grand piano
Clothing piles on the floor
Propped on her elbows
she sips wine
He expertly plays music
filling the air
Her hands move sensually
on her breasts
Their eyes lock smoky and intense

She parts her stocking clad legs
Hands on her abdomen then
to her silky fold
Intentionally she spills
wine onto her mound
Fingering herself entering then out
She writhes as she pleasures herself

Fully arouse he took her lips
Then strokes her satiny skin
Each stroke a note to a song
She is divine and grander
than the instrument
He enjoys the taste of the wine
soft meet sweet

His fingers replace hers
enter her heat

Moans and quivers
she is ready for him
Now bare he pulls her
to the edge of the piano
Swiftly he fills her
with his masculinity
-River Stone

TEMPTRESS

Gentle waves crawled
to the deserted beach shore
The temptress whispered
her voice sexy and sultry
She climbed onto his lap
each moves slow and sensual
Firm legs wrapped him
as she bounced lightly
Her full firm pendulous breasts
filled his vision

Hands by his sides fully
aroused he enjoyed the show
She continued to tease hips
swaying legs spread
Exposed crotchless lace panties
as she fingered herself
Her hot wet crotch massaged
his throbbing hardness
Calculated moves from
an experience seductress

Legs ajar he felt her heat
the temptation was too strong
Like a hungry beast
he entered and penetrated her depth

-River Stone

WILD SIDE

She sits on a rock
wearing no undies
Her legs opening
and closing slowly
Mischievous smile
frames her face
She turns her head
to meet his gaze
With one stride he
joins her on the rock

He crushes her mouth
kissing her deeply
He caresses and molds
exposed skin
Hands touches
her femininity
At the side of a trail
without cover
The risk did not quell
their desire

No prolong foreplay
as they ache
Blanket taken from
his hiking bag

Spreads on the rock
forming a cushion
On her hands and knees
she is eager and ready
He thrust firmly
panting like an animal
Her side to side wriggles
urges him on
Moans echo in the wild
audile from afar
The tornado builds
from the tip of toes
Voices heard in the distance
still no abort
Ecstasy beats out
reasoning and logics
The voices drew closer
as they explode
Time to pull down
her dress and close his zipper

-River Stone

ON TOP OF THE TABLE

Crush against
his masculine frame
Like an orchestra
her body screams
Matching each kiss
as fierce as his
Body in heat like
a lone caged tigress
He lifts her onto
the table and swiftly
Lacey pieces rips off
she is now naked

He is well endowed
she begs for him to enter
Hungrily he licks and
she melts like butter
He pulls her to the edge
then slides into her oasis
She rocks her hips
side to side as he pumps
Grabbing the table as
she enjoys a violent orgasm

-River Stone

SHARED PLEASURE
Entwine head to toe
in sixty-nine
Tongue spreads
her delicate lips
Skillfully invading
her eager slit

Loving the taste and
scent of her body
Reciprocating she strokes
his length
One jewel then the other
in her mouth
Licking and kissing
she gives pleasure
His hearts races as
his blood sets ablaze
Fingers probes
her pool of moisture

Feverish she shakes
oh, this is insane
Shaft into her mouth
she draws like candy
Unevenly he breathes
as he curls his toes

Head over heels
they satisfy each other
Each lost
in the depth of their desire
        -River Stone

THE LAP DANCE

She guides him
to sit on a chair
Wearing tiny shorts
stiletto on her feet
Running her palm
over his naked torso
Straddling him while
he still wears boxers

Gliding her crotch
onto is erected member
He tenses as
his heartbeats quicken
Her hips move
in a circular motion
He caresses her breasts
draped in lace

Sliding out of her shorts
seductively and sensually
Still clad in panties
she grinds him with wet heat
Backward forward she rocks
him a sweltering furnace
Hard and throbbing
he grabs her butt

Gyrating her hips
she knows he needs release
He rips off
her tiny lace fabric
And sink deep
in her pulsating abyss
Excitement of his release
drove her to her own peak
            -River Stone

THE MIRROR

He took her from behind
Bypassing the foreplay
She was already soaking wet
Fast intense freaking hot

Their skin glistened with sweat
The reflection in the mirror
Damn it was a sight to see
Better than an adult movie

Stirred his desire even more
He attacked her pulsating heat
Panting shaking and exploding
The mirror told the fiery tale
                -River Stone

AT THE CLUB

He winked and her eyes cast down
There was no hiding the huge bulge
Zipper straining needed relief
Playfully she patted the hardened
spot
The air charred and his mouth
parched
A quickie would certainly be
satisfying

Yearning drove him senselessly
insane
His husky whisper told her the tale
Aching needing to be one with her
Provocatively she bumped and
grinded him
Mischief and intending to torture in
mind
She reached back and fondled his
crotch
A few more drinks would be so
unwise
Minus inhibitions they would do it
there tonight

-River Stone

THE CAPTIVE

Clothes loosely scattered making a
trail to the bedroom
Evidently someone has disrobed in a
hurry
She is clad in leather bikini top and
bottom
Knee-high leather boots hug her
shapely calves
Hair pulls tight at the top of her
head
covered by a 1940s soldier's hat

Standing tall legs apart
whip in hand hangs by her side
It is clear who is in charge
as she smacks the daylight out of
her lover
He is now a fish out of water
bitter sweet there is no retreat

He is still cuffed but she removes
the blind fold
Covers his body in oil tenderly
massaging
His weapon thick and hard stands
tall

Yearns for the attention of his lady
soldier
Her captive has no control
completely he surrenders
Her fingers slide in through the side
of skimpy leather
Simultaneously her tongue makes
love to his member
Up down he is a furnace as he
howls like a wild wolf anxious for
mating
Provocatively she removes the tiny
leather pieces
And with a pull of pins her long
tresses cascade down her back
hat discarded

He eyed the feast gosh she was
more than a treat
Breathtakingly beautiful and
spontaneous she keeps him
guessing, always exciting
She lowers herself on his throbbing
master piece
Rocking to and fro as she rides her
beast
Eyes close she strokes her naked
hot breasts

The captive is in heaven growling
and shuddering
She rides with full control of her
speed her moans soft purrs
Here comes her explosion, fireworks
behind close lids
The ride does not stop until he
explodes and have his moment
Fulfilled they lie in each other arms
as his fingers comb her long silky
tresses
                    -River Stone

COCOONED

Her moist flower opened
I entered and was enfolded in her
cocoon
Overwhelmed with emotions my
eyes
became pools that spilled over on
my cheeks
I was in love
-River Stone

DRUNK DESIRE

Girl you are under my skin
Have to confess I am addicted
Love when you blush under my
stare
When I use my eyes to remove your
dress
Dangerously sexy your moves stir
my loin
Alluring hypnotic I have eyes only
for you

Body temperature elevates from
naked want
Shaking gasping need to catch my
breath
Dizzy and defenseless when our
bodies collide
Intoxicating attraction just cannot
deny
I want to sweat from our passionate
grind
And take you to unimaginable
heights

-River Stone

FANTASY NIGHT
Starry night full moon
and us two lovers
The backyard garden
a nest of splendor
Fire burns in your eyes
passion no doubt
Our lips meet
oh, sweet surrender

Breasts expose
to the cool midnight air
You arch your back and
give me a mouth full
Your tantalizing scents
massages my nostrils
Making love to you
bare under my touch

A glass of wine
destroys all inhibitions
My eyes worship you
beautiful so sexy
You spread your legs
to give full access
My fingers glide
into your moist heat

Breathless you are ready
to be one with me
Moans are loud
and very unapologetic
I stare into the moon
this is heaven
Thrusting and meeting
your every rhythm
We climax fulfilling
our backyard fantasies
-River Stone

VOLCANOES ERUPT

Eyes close I think of you
I won the jackpot
you are my prize
My pursuit was
intense and deliberate
Still I am amaze
you chose to be with me
Alluring intoxicating
you are my flaming desire
Senselessly crazy
head over heels for you
I need you so much
it is indescribable
Eyes open I reach for you
I pull you close and
stroke your velvet skin
Staring in your eyes
searching your soul
Roving hands cups your peaks
until nipples harden
Then travels to your valley
finding the moist retreat
Stirring the pot
I know this is driving you wild

Eyes dark with desire

I yearn for you
I lick your juices
from my wet fingers
On my back you
Eagerly straddle me
While you ride
your breast fills my mouth
Writhing bouncing
your tightness grips my shaft
Scandalous moans escape us
as our volcanoes erupt
-River Stone

NAKED DESIRE
She lay naked on a bed of rose
At the blazing sight I was arouse
I did not need any other invitation
It was all in her expression
I quickly disrobed
And penetrated her fold
-River Stone

GODDESS

Her condo is parallel
across from mine
Sadly, I am in love but our
relationship is platonic
We say hello, share small talks
and exchange smiles
Tonight, I watch her from my
window through my telescope

Draped in lingerie
stilettos and garter belt
Sipping from a wine glass
she sensually dances
Each move seductive
I wonder if she knows I watch
Legs open I get a glimpse
of her luscious heaven

Pinching the areola
of each globe in her full bosom
She parts her lips and
fingers the junction of her thigh
Gyrating her hips
hand to her mouth she tastes
her honeypot
Then she reaches for a lucky toy

and sink it into her moist nest
Oh, I wish that toy was me
  -River Stone

DREAMING

I watch you sleep
hope you dream of me
The contour of your face
perfectly set
Almond shape eyes
behind close lids
Cute dent at the
ridge of your nose

Velvety soft skin I adore
Your hair glistens
under the light glow
The rise and fall of
your breasts excite
Angelic smile frames
your face so divine
Radiant and astonishing
your beauty amazes

I pull you close and
hear your heartbeats
You are safe protected
with me my love
You occupy my head
I am daydreaming of
your kisses each sweeter

than the other
Whisper of your voice
calming yet arousing
You stroke my frame
with your smooth hands
Tantalizing touch
caressing intimate parts
Temperature rising
anxiety builds

You move I move
our breathing uneven
Hardness against softness
nut meets bolt
Heartbeats slowly
return to an even pace
       -River Stone

NOT A ONE NIGHT STAND
I watch her all night and
conclude she is alone
Alluring radiant tempting
the belle of the ball
Sexy shapely legs
I would love to be between
Dazzling is her smile
from across the room
With deliberate
quick strides I am by her side

Honeyed voice says her name
I am in a trance
Vanilla peach orange basil
loving her scent
Guides her to the dance floor
happy she accepts
Heart skips a few beats
shamelessly I am aroused
In our own world we sway
to the music needing more

Whispers huskily and
she follows me to the stairwell
Kiss her like a hunger beast
so delicious and fragrant

Caress and suckle her
sumptuous breasts to her delight
Want to rip off her panties
but I am a gentleman tonight
Pulls them over her ankles and
fingers her wet flower

I pause to sheath my harden rod
protecting us both
Her legs wrap my waist as
I enter into her sweet heat
Bouncing up and down
the wild tigress rides my pole
Staring into her passion scorch eyes
a powerful connection
Gripping the curve of her
perfect buttocks I pump faster
Electricity gash through
my body as I howl and groan
I hold on until she is there too
then we explode together
Silence except for our
thumping hearts
Definitely she is for keeps
      -River Stone

ONE NIGHT STAND
Handsome sexy with
a cute boyish grin
Perfect teeth flashes
from across the room
Tone legs took long
strides to be by my side
The discovery of his
appealing arousing voice
He says more than hello
but I did not hear much

Lost staring at him
magnificent hunk of a man
He asks for my name and
I am jolt back to earth
Warm hand on my back
he leads me to the dance floor
Cannot deny I am glad
to be single and free to mingle
Undeniable the attraction
he peaks my attention

Against good judgment
I follow him to the stairwell
No time to waste as
he nails me against the wall

My little black dress
forms a pool at my waist
As swift hands pull
my panties over my ankles
Oh, my goodness this is
my first one-night stand!

Hands knead my breasts and
fondle my hot wetness
Legs around his waist
his arousal fills my essence
Our eyes lock as he
rhythmically thrust in and out
Fireworks in my head as
we climax, wow my first orgasm!
Limp and spent we hold each other
as our breathing slow

Fast forward many years
we remain together, sweet lover
I will never forget
that super amazing night we met
       -River Stone

LIGHT MY FIRE

Stroke me with your fingers
And knead my shapely breasts
Crush my softness with your hard
chest
Quench my thirst as our tongues
tango
Lick my essence make me shiver
Lubricate my nub make me wet
Light my fire drive me wild

Part my legs plunge your hardness
Fill me with the length tip to base
Move with me thrust for thrust
Hit my G-spot from all angles
Make me moan groan and whimper
Hold me tight when we explode
And whisper you love me
       -River Stone

SWEET TORTURE
I licked my lips
to start the wicked tease
Lips trailed a path
of kisses to your neck
The base throbbed
evidence of your arousal

Hands travelled in circles
on your hard chest
Small circles faded
into larger ones
Nipples were pinched
pleasure was the intent
You were breathless
the desired reaction
Lips followed hands
tongue followed lips
Damn you were sexy!
Damn you smelled so good!

My tongue painted
abstract art on your body
Perfectly manicured fingers
brushed your length
More kisses a pause at the
ridge of the pubic bone

You writhed and tried to
hoist yourself above the bed
Hungry for more, restricted
by the dark red handcuffs
Heart was pounding, temperature
rose as my hands pumped

Full control of your
shaft up down repeat
You begged wanted needed more
oh, sweet torture!
      -River Stone

FIERY DESIRE

Our lips met
the battle of the lips began
You kissed me
hungrily I moaned and groaned

My breasts crushed
against your muscular frame
Heart beat quickened
a furnace between my legs

Hands roamed
over my body my blood boils
Kneaded caressed
I was still starving for more

You gripped
my sweet triangle cladded in lace
Probed my intimate
oh my God this was insane

My head
was spinning I was on fire
Then you pulled
me closer entering my eager nest
I quivered and loved you some more

    -River Stone

OVER THE CLIFF

Passionate kisses
as you drink my sweetness
You devour my tongue
groans escape your throat

My lip travels
the distance to your organ
It stands at attention
begging to be touch

Swiftly I wipe
the pre-come from the tip
My tongue slides
into the small opening
Salty yet delicious!
What a treat!

Sexy fingers form
a cocoon around the shaft
To your delight
I lick your jewels

Firm and hard
in my mouth you almost explode
Your toes curl
orchestra going off in your head

I bring you to the edge
and back then over the cliff
        -River Stone

74

MAGICAL FINGERS

I was fully aroused
anxious for what you offered
I wanted your full
harden length deep inside me
captivating driving me
to that point of no return
Panties ripped off
and your knee separated my legs

You fondled my center
my juice all over your fingers
Wet fingers massaged
my clit my moans pervaded the
room
Without warning
two fingers were inside my honeypot
I was hot and eager
but you had other plans

My walls clenched the fingers
taking all pleasure
Back arched legs spread
I shamelessly begged for more
Two fingers became three
crafts man you are skilled
Doubled the pleasure

as your thumb work on my clit
I gyrated my hips
who knew your fingers were magical

You continued the act
in and out and in again
Rhythmic fingers
increased their speed
Juices gushed
from my body rocked by shock
waves
                    -River Stone

DANGEROUS DESIRE
Click it's your key
in the door
You have been with her
again, for sure
You love me you hurt me
then repeat
My pain has numbed
sleep evades me
Crystal clear your
deceptive smile
Lame excuses playing
with my mind

You head for the shower
While the pillow
muffles my sobs
Dangerously handsome
and irresistible
In your arms your lips
crush mine
My deceptive body
comes alive
It again lets me down

You rip off my nightdress
and whispers beautiful sexy

your voice husky
Your mouth hot
hands roaming
My back arches
yearning for more
My biggest sin
is loving you
You are addictive
Intoxicating

Stir of my heat
I am on fire
Thrusts into my depth
I fall apart
Moaning groaning
screaming your name
The climax worth the misery
-River Stone

TALK TO ME DIRTY

You fill my head
consuming my thoughts
Spellbinding tantalizing
and dirty thoughts
Mad about you longing
to kiss your plummy lips

I want you as the entree
serve me your platter
As you walk in the door
discard your pants
Stroke me gently with
your callus hands

Let me taste your cocktail
every last drop
There are no plans
to have a bun in my oven
So, before that wild ride
sheath your rod

Talk to me dirty
as you enter my drenched slit
I look forward to
a marathon several furlongs
Gasping hot wet and

euphoric as you hit the spot
-River Stone

LOVER BOY

Sexy rugged charming
I was attracted
Fell in love with
his creative mind his
Easy-going persona
funny and unassuming
I became addicted
after the first rendezvous

He touched me with
heavenly agility
His kisses hot and juicy
quenched my thirst
The tongue was magical
he is a master
My cherry swelled
With each lick I climbed the wall

Lover lit a fire
between my legs I burned
His sturdy rod
stirred my eager pot
I gave five-star rating
for his lovemaking
Lover boy could toot his horn
there was no comparison

-River Stone

LET US PLAY TONIGHT

Let's flirt and tease to start
Stroke my hills valley every inch
I want you to taste my cookie
Lick me until my juice oozes

Then finger my hot wet honeypot
Enter with your thick firm length
My tight walls will grip your shaft
Make me breathless gasping and
trembling

Thrust in and out while I ride
Clenching guarantee it will be wild
Come with me as I explode
Under the flickering candle light
-River Stone

INTOXICATING SPELL

I am under
your intoxicating spell
Your sweltering
stare ignites my fire
Peel my covers
I want to be bare
Strum me with your fingers
Knead my voluptuous peaks

Crush my softness
with your hard torso
Quench my thirst as
our tongues entwine
Lick my intimate heat
make me creamy
Then lubricate
my pink pearl with my juice
Work magic with your thumb
tease with the index

Be my surgeon
your shaft and lips your tools
Legs parted that is the invitation
Slide your member
plug my tightness
Gift me your full-length

your entire package
Quench me as intensity peaks

Flip me over
to my favorite position
Double the pleasure
on my hands and knees
Hit my sweet spot
left right and center
Satisfy my appetite
it is climax I seek
Electrifying mind-blowing
sweet release
        -River Stone

ABOUT THE AUTHOR

River Stone enjoys writing steamy tales.

She lives in Ontario, Canada. Loves to cozy up with a glass of wine on the sofa reading romantic poems, novels and watching movies.

River finds it interesting to attend food festivals in the great multicultural city of Toronto, savoring the various flavors and meeting new people.

She hopes you enjoy reading **Sweet and Fiery Erotic Love Poems** over and over again.

Another book by the author that you may enjoy:

TRULY THE ONE – (A love story)

www.ingramcontent.com/pod-product-compliance
Lightning Source LLC
Chambersburg PA
CBHW051003050726
47592CB00007B/2686